W9-AVK-610

Published in 2016 by **Windmill Books**,
an Imprint of Rosen Publishing
29 East 21st Street, New York, NY 10010

Copyright © 2016 Blake Publishing

Principal photographer: Narinda Sandry
Additional photography: Dreamstime; Greg Harm:
front cover (silkworm), pp. 9–11, 22, IBC (silkworm); Steve
Parish/Nature-Connect: pp. 3, 5 (sheep), 8, 18, 19 (dam), 20;
Ken Stepnell: pp. 7 (sheep), 23 (sheep flock).
Photo research: Emma Harm
Cover and text design: Leanne Nobilio
Color management: Greg Harm
Editor: Vanessa Barker

Library of Congress Cataloging-in-Publication Data
Johnson, Rebecca.
Sophie the silkworm / by Rebecca Johnson.
p. cm. — (Bug Adventures)
Includes index.
ISBN 978-1-4777-5621-8 (pbk.)
ISBN 978-1-4777-5620-1 (6 pack)
ISBN 978-1-4777-5544-0 (library binding)
1. Silkworms — Juvenile literature.
I. Johnson, Rebecca, 1966-. II. Title.
SF542.5 J683 2016
638—d23

Manufactured in the United States of America
CPSIA Compliance Information: Batch WS15WM: For Further Information
contact Rosen Publishing, New York, New York at 1-800-237-9932

BUG ADVENTURES

CONTENTS

Sophie the
silkworm sat
on a mulberry
leaf listening to a
flock of sheep talking.

"We are so important," said one sheep. "I don't know what humans would do without us," said another.

All the other sheep
agreed that they
were very important.
Sophie nodded and agreed too.
Wool was special. It was used to make
socks, sweaters, and all sorts of things.

"I am important to humans too,"
said Sophie, wanting to join in.
The sheep looked around.
"Did you hear
something?"
said an old ewe.

I'm over here!

5

"It was me!" called Sophie in her tiny voice. "I said I was important too. My silk is used to make clothes, sheets, ropes, and even bulletproof vests!"

The sheep looked up at the leaf where Sophie sat. "Baaaaa!" they burst out laughing together. "I think you might be confused, dear," said the ewe.

Baaaaa!

Baaaaa!

"I am not,"
said the silkworm.
"My silk is just as important as your wool."
"How could a little worm like you be
any use at all?" snapped the ram.

"I am NOT a worm," said Sophie. "I am the larva of a moth, and one day I will show you how important my silk is."

"I'd like to see that," laughed the ram, and the sheep walked away.

Sophie started to eat. She ate as fast as she could.

The faster she ate, the faster she grew. She grew so fast, she shed her skin four times.

She would
show them
all. Her friends
ate as fast as
they could too.

When they could not eat any more, they began to spin their cocoons. Each cocoon was made from one long piece of silk.

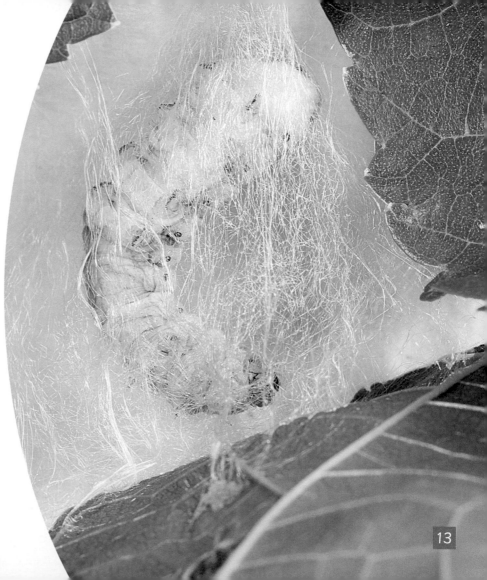

Around and around
they went, until
each silkworm
was hidden
inside.

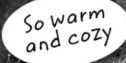

zzzz zzzz zzzz zzzz

They stayed like this
for two to three weeks.

15

At last, the fat,
white moths emerged.

They found mates,
laid their eggs,
and then
they died.

The sheep didn't
give Sophie
a second
thought.

Then, one day,
an awful thing
happened.
The old ram fell
into the pond and
could not get out.

"Quick," called the farmer to his son, "get a rope! Get the really strong one."

"Get the silk rope. It's light and strong but soft, so it won't hurt the ram when we pull him out."

Even though the ram was scared, all he could think about was how he had treated Sophie and how the silk that she spoke of was now going to save his life.

When he was finally pulled free, he made sure he told every sheep in his flock that silk was just as useful as wool...

...even though it came from a tiny little silkworm, who was not a worm at all.

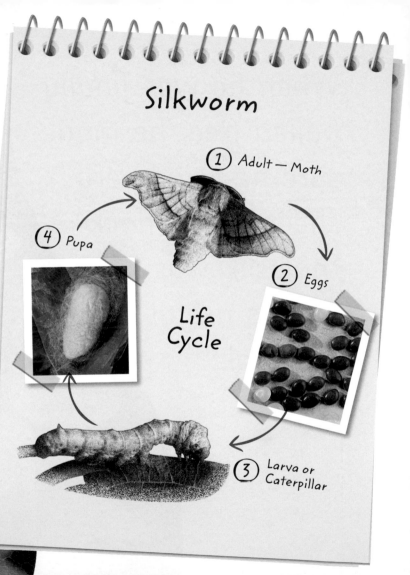